BENNY
FINDS A HOME

written by: Cheryl Johnson

t publishing
CHILDREN'S DIVISION

Published by Tate Publishing & Enterprises, LLC
127 E. Trade Center Terrace | Mustang, Oklahoma 73064 USA
1.888.361.9473 | www.tatepublishing.com

Tate Publishing is committed to excellence in the publishing industry. The company reflects the philosophy established by the founders, based on Psalm 68:11,
"The Lord gave the word and great was the company of those who published it."

Book design copyright © 2015 by Tate Publishing, LLC. All rights reserved.
Cover and interior design by Eileen Cueno
Illustrations by Marivir Lynn Lomocso

Published in the United States of America

ISBN: 978-1-68237-224-1
Juvenile Fiction / Religious / Christian / Animals
15.09.11

THIS BOOK BELONGS TO:

_____

For Jayelyn —
One of my very favorite
nieces!
Love you bunches!
Aunt Cheryl

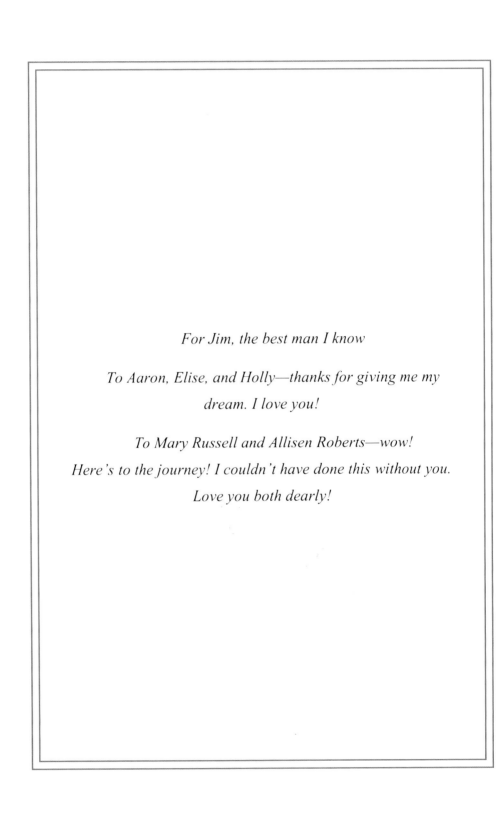

For Jim, the best man I know

To Aaron, Elise, and Holly—thanks for giving me my
dream. I love you!

To Mary Russell and Allisen Roberts—wow!
Here's to the journey! I couldn't have done this without you.
Love you both dearly!

Bentley scooted the toy bone around Farmer Tom and Mrs. Nettie's kitchen as fast as his stout, little legs and his small, pudgy nose would let him. Then he would suddenly run to the back door with the clear glass in it, tilt his head one way, then the other, and finally go back to scooting his toy bone. Bentley was trying to be patient, but it was getting more difficult every day! *"All my brother and sister puppies have found their families, and they all have children to play with! When is my family coming to get me? Why am I the last one here?"* Bentley wondered.

For the past couple of weeks, families would show up at the house, play with all the little puppies, and suddenly declare their love for their chosen one. But they hadn't picked Bentley, and he knew he just had to have a child of his very own!

"Why not me?" Bentley thought. *"Don't they think I am playful enough? Maybe I am too small! Or maybe it's my fur— all black with tufts of red here and there! If only I was golden blonde like my sister,"* he pondered.

Bentley remembered hearing Farmer Tom praying to God, thanking Him and asking for things he wanted. Bentley thought it was worth giving God a try. Bentley closed his eyes tightly and imagined his prayer to God.

"Dear Most Gracious Heavenly Father, who art in heaven..."

That was how Farmer Tom always started his prayers, and he wanted to be as official as possible! He couldn't mess this up!

"*I would really like a family of my own,*" Bentley continued. "*One with some children to play with. I'll behave. I promise. You know - just a nice little family that I can help. Thank you. Amen!*"

Bentley thought that was a pretty good prayer and hoped God was listening.

Bentley had no idea how God was working on just the perfect family for him or how badly another family needed him.

Across town, Aaron, Elise, and Holly were just arriving home from school.

"How was school today, Holly?" her mother asked as Holly came dragging in.

"Same as it is every day. Horrible!" Holly moaned as she sat down to eat a snack.

During the summer, Holly's family had moved to a new home, in a new town, in a new state. Her dad had joined the staff at the Hope Bible Church.

"Each day will get better," Mom told her. "I promise."

Holly just stared at her. Neither was sure if Holly really believed that, but Mom prayed every day for her, and Mom believed it. Holly was just having a hard time with change.

Aaron and Elise didn't seem to mind moving. They always seemed to make friends easily. Holly tried making friends at school, but it was hard. All the girls seemed to already know each other, and Holly felt like an outsider.

Holly learned what it meant to ask Jesus into her heart last Christmas. At the end of a Christmas play, the pastor talked about why Jesus was born. On the ride home, Holly asked about what Bro. Bruce said that night.

Holly's mom explained, "We all do things that are wrong. We must be sorry for the things we do and follow Jesus. Remember when you learned the ABC's of becoming a Christian?"

"Yes," Holly answered.

"*A*, admit I've done wrong. *B*, believe Jesus came to die for my sins. *C*, commit my life to Him."

"That's right," Mom said. "That's the real meaning of being a Christian, and I hope one day you'll want to follow Jesus."

Holly decided right then what to do and said, "I want to follow Jesus, and I have to do it right now." That night she prayed with her parents and decided to follow Jesus always.

Holly knew Jesus would take care of her, but she had a lot of questions she wanted to ask God. She wandered outside to her swing where she could think. Slowly, she began winding up that swing like a screw in a piece of wood, tighter and tighter. As she twisted, the questions started coming. She whispered them at first, but when that swing was fully wound, she felt like she was shouting.

"God, wouldn't it be okay to have a friend here that I could see and hear and talk to. And why am I the only one who seems so lonely? Is it asking too much to have at least *one* friend?"

When Dad came home that night, Mom told him about an idea she had. Holly didn't know it, but her parents began talking about getting a little puppy to help with her loneliness.

On Saturday, Holly came moping into the kitchen as usual.

"Holly, how would you like to get a puppy?" Mom asked.

"What?" Holly squealed. "Are you serious? But it's not my birthday or Christmas or anything!"

"Well," Mom started, "the puppy would be a family dog, but you would have to take care of it. Can you do that?"

"Oh yes, Mom! I can!" Holly promised.

Mom smiled as she said, "We'll have to find the right puppy. You can start looking on this website."

Holly eagerly scrolled through the adorable images of the puppies. Elise heard the commotion coming from the kitchen and quickly joined in the search.

It wasn't long before a beautiful little puppy whose black fur dotted with tufts of red was staring his black puppy dog eyes right into the faces of Holly and Elise. Their hearts fluttered as they gazed at this adorable little puppy.

"Mom!" they cried together. "We found him! And his name is Bentley!"

Elise and Holly glanced at each other for a quick second, and then Holly cried, "Mom, call now! Pleeease!"

Mom laughed, and the girls looked at each other confused. Then Mom said, "I fell in love with Bentley too when I looked through the ads this morning. So I took a chance and decided to call. We've got an appointment at 2! We'd better get going!"

Holly didn't realize it, but God was working on answering her questions.

Holly and Elise could hardly believe it! They laughed as they ran to get their shoes. When they ran passed their brother's room, they called out, "Hey! We're going to get a puppy. Wanna come?"

Aaron had heard the rumours of a puppy, but he didn't actually believe them. This he had to see.

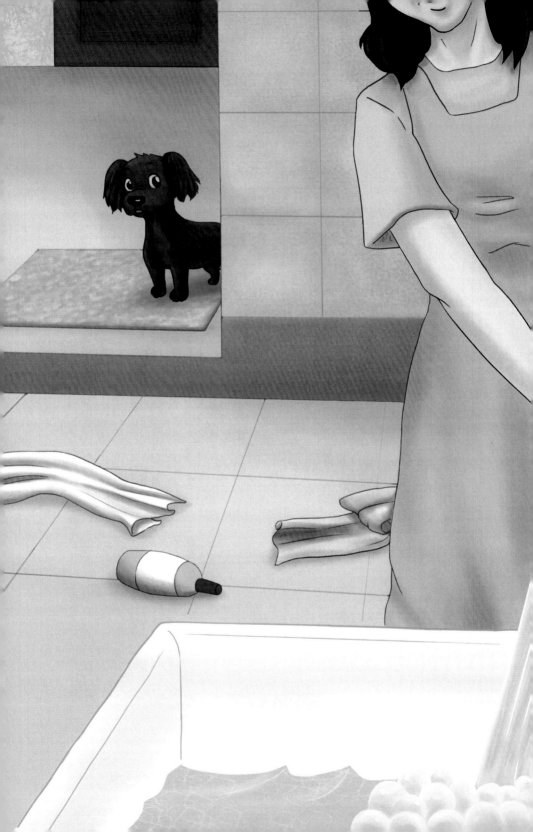

Bentley woke up from his nap to the sound of water splashing. Mrs. Nettie was filling the bathtub with water. *"I wonder what she's doing?"* he thought to himself as he started to prance away. But before he could get very far, he was scooped up and placed in that tub. *"What's happening?"* he wondered. He was lathered up and rinsed off. By the time he thought he might like it, he felt a giant towel swoosh him up and shake him around. For a moment, he thought he was going to be tossed away, but then he felt his tummy get tickled, and he couldn't help but laugh.

Finally, Bentley was put on the ground, and he heard Mrs. Nettie say, "Now you're all nice and clean! And you smell handsome too! Like a little man! The family that's coming to meet you today will just fall in love with you!"

"Family? Did she say family?"

Bentley hoped he heard her correctly.

Suddenly Bentley was full of doubts. *"What if the family doesn't love me? What if they see my tufts of red and think it's ugly or they think I am too small?"*

Bentley decided he should pray one more time.

"Dear Most Gracious Heavenly Father, who art in heaven," he started. *"Please help this family love me. And help me be good. Amen."*

Bentley took his place at the back door in the kitchen and tried to be patient. Soon Bentley heard the wheels of a car whirring down the driveway. He could hardly contain his excitement.

Holly, Elise, and Aaron came barrelling out of the car almost before their mother could bring it to a complete stop.

Holly scooped Bentley up and took him to her mom. "Look, Mom, he's perfect! Isn't he beautiful? His fur is so pretty, and he's just the right size. Can we keep him? Pleeease?"

"Yes, dear!" Mom exclaimed. "I do believe Bentley was meant for us!"

Bentley was as happy as Holly to hear this and started smothering Holly with puppy dog kisses!

Bentley loved his new home and explored each room, sniffing everything. Bentley was glad he had prayed. God *had* found the perfect home for him!

The next morning he overheard Holly and her mom talking about how sad Holly had been. Bentley knew he had to work hard to make Holly feel special.

Later that day, Holly was taking Bentley for a walk. Bentley was sniffing his short little nose along the street when he realized he was sniffing another dog. He began barking so loudly that he didn't even notice there were two other kids with the dog he was having a barking contest with!

"Hush!" Holly scolded him.

"Oh! What a cute little puppy!" The voice was coming from the girl holding the leash of an equally cute little puppy!

"Thanks!" Holly replied.

"I'm Janie," the girl said, "and this is my brother Jay. We live down the street. You're new here, right?"

"Yeah," said Holly shyly. "We've lived here a few months."

"What's your dog's name?" questioned Jay.

"It's Bentley," said Holly. "But we usually just call him Benny."

"Cool," said Jay. "Well, this is Roxie. Do you and Benny want to walk with us?"

"Sure," said Holly.

They hadn't gotten far when a white dog with long, brown floppy ears and her nose low to the ground came running up to them, dragging her leash. No owner was in sight!

This new dog set Benny and Roxie both off, even though this dog was four times their size!

Holly squealed with delight. "It's a hush puppy! A hound dog!"

Jay bent down to scratch the hush puppy's long ears to try to make friends and to protect Roxie and Benny.

Just then they all heard a girl's voice yelling sharply, "Penny? Peeennnyyy!"

Janie shouted back, "I think your dog's over here!"

"Oh, thanks," the girl said with relief. "I was walking her, and she got away!"

Just then Aaron came racing down the street with Elise following close behind. "Hey, Missy!" Aaron said. "So this is your dog, huh?"

"Sure is!" Missy replied.

"She's as big as you!" Aaron teased.

Elise and Holly gave Aaron a funny look, so Aaron said, "We go to school together!"

As Elise and Holly were rolling their eyes, Jay exclaimed, "We were just headed to the park. Is everybody in?"

The group that had grown continued down the street. Aaron, Elise, and Missy, still trying to get Penny to follow along, led the way. Janie, Jay, and Holly, with Roxie and Benny in tow, followed behind, laughing and talking quite excitedly.

At one point, Holly bent down to scratch Benny's ears and said, "Thanks, Benny! Thanks for helping me make new friends." Then whispering, she added, "And thank you, God. Thank you for always being there for me!"

Benny said a little prayer to himself too. "*Thank you, God, for giving me this wonderful family. And I'm sorry for barking at those other dogs. I'll try to do better!*" Benny was smiling as he trotted along, happy that he had helped Holly make some new friends and that God had given him this wonderful family.

The most important thing that happened to Holly wasn't getting a new puppy or making new friends. It was asking Jesus into her heart. Is that something you have done? Holly talked about the ABC's of becoming a Christian. You may already know those, but just in case, here they are again:

A – Admit that you are a sinner.

This just means that you have done something wrong. Nobody is perfect except God and Jesus. We all mess up! (Romans 3:23, Romans 6:23, Niv)

B – Believe that Jesus is God's Son. He died for you so you could live forever in heaven with Him.

Do you like to get presents? I do! God gave us the best present ever. All we have to do is believe in Jesus and accept Him. We will still have hard times like Holly, but God will always be there to help us. (John 3:16, John 14:6, Niv)

C – Confess your sins and tell Jesus that you want to follow Him.

Isn't it hard to admit when you're wrong? It's easier to blame someone else or just say you didn't do it. But we have to admit that we do wrong things and ask God to forgive us so we can follow God. And every time we ask, God always forgives. God loves you very much! (Romans 10:9–10, Niv)

e|LIVE

listen|imagine|view|experience

AUDIO BOOK DOWNLOAD INCLUDED WITH THIS BOOK!

In your hands you hold a complete digital entertainment package. In addition to the paper version, you receive a free download of the audio version of this book. Simply use the code listed below when visiting our website. Once downloaded to your computer, you can listen to the book through your computer's speakers, burn it to an audio CD or save the file to your portable music device (such as Apple's popular iPod) and listen on the go!

How to get your free audio book digital download:

1. Visit www.tatepublishing.com and click on the e|LIVE logo on the home page.
2. Enter the following coupon code:
   2b63-4a9d-1546-9167-ca1a-a367-b1bf-7931
3. Download the audio book from your e|LIVE digital locker and begin enjoying your new digital entertainment package today!